INCREDIBLE
INSECTS Q&A

Written by Sally Tagholm

Consultant Dr. George C. McGavin

DK

LONDON, NEW YORK,
MELBOURNE, MUNICH, AND DELHI

Senior Art Editor Sheila Collins
Designer Joanne Little
Senior Editor Fran Jones
Managing Editor Linda Esposito
Managing Art Editor Diane Thistlethwaite
Publishing Manager Andrew Macintyre
Category Publisher Laura Buller
Design Development Manager Sophia M. Tampakopoulos
Production Editors Laragh Kedwell, Vivianne Ridgeway
DK Picture Library Claire Bowers, Rose Horridge
Picture Research Myriam Mégharbi
Jacket Editor Mariza O'Keeffe
Jacket Designer Laura Brim
US Editor Margaret Parrish

First published in the United States in 2009
by DK Publishing
375 Hudson Street, New York, New York 10014

Copyright © 2009 Dorling Kindersley Limited

09 10 11 12 13 10 9 8 7 6 5 4 3 2 1
BD712 – 04/09

A catalog record for this book is available
from the Library of Congress.

ISBN 978-0-7566-5193-0

Printed and bound in China by Hung Hing

Discover more at
www.dk.com

CONTENTS

WHAT IS AN INSECT?

When is a bug not a bug?

Many people think that "bugs" is a word that describes all insects, but this is not the case. Only one group of insects can be called bugs, and the correct term for them is "true bugs." Insects, part of a larger grouping known as arthropods, make up more than half of all animal species on Earth, and some—such as dragonflies—have been around since before the time of the dinosaurs. To study them better, scientists organize insects that share key features into groups, called orders. Butterflies and moths are just one of the seven main orders shown here.

One of butterfly's six legs

Head with compound eyes

Antenna

Q A What is a true bug?

There are several distinguishing features of a true bug. Most have forewings that are divided into two and that overlap when folded. They also have specialized piercing mouthparts. Since true bugs are unable to chew their food, they stab prey with a sharp beak and inject it with saliva that liquefies tissue. Then they suck up this soft part of the victim's body.

Queen Alexandra's birdwing butterfly

Bug's beak injects poison into prey

Ground beetle prey

Assassin bug

Q A Which is the largest order of insect?

Beetles easily make up the largest order of insect. They come in a range of shapes and sizes but share one distinctive feature—a toughened set of forewings, known as elytra. Many beetles are dull-colored but others are bright and shiny.

Forewing

Hindwing

Abdomen

Grasshopper

More Facts

■ Hawk moths are among the fastest-flying insects. Some can fly at 33 mph (53 km/h).

Giant hawk moth

■ Tiger beetles are one of the fastest-running insects and can reach speeds of 8 ft per second (2.5 m per second).

■ There are roughly 82,000 species of true bug in the world.

■ One in three animal species on the planet is a beetle.

■ One species of stick insect has the longest body of all insects. Females can be 22 in (55 cm), full length.

Q A Can insects sing?
Grasshoppers and crickets have sturdy bodies, two pairs of well-developed wings, and extra-large back legs. To attract their mates, male crickets sing by rubbing their front wings together. Some male grasshoppers produce a song by rubbing their hind legs against their folded wings.

Q A Are ants related to wasps?
Yes, they are. Bees, wasps, and ants fall into the same insect order, and almost all have two pairs of wings and a narrow waist. While bees feed on pollen and nectar, ants and wasps eat a range of food.

House fly

Wasp

Q A How does a fly know where to land?
True flies have sense organs on their feet, which they use to "taste" things they land on—an excellent way of finding food. House flies have "claws" and sticky pads on their feet so that they can cling to flat surfaces and walk upside down.

Golden scarab beetle

Q A How many legs does a dragonfly have?
Like all insects, dragonflies and damselflies have six jointed legs. They have long bodies, large eyes, and two pairs of transparent wings. Unlike most insects, a dragonfly's wings beat in opposite directions, so it can hover in midair and fly backward.

Elytron

Dragonfly

Do bees have brains?

All adult insects share the same basic body plan, no matter what size they are. They have three main parts—a head, a thorax, and an abdomen, where most of the internal organs are tightly packed. The brain is located in the head and receives messages from sense organs. A bumble bee, as shown here, has a relatively small brain with about 950,000 brain cells (humans have 100 billion). Insects also have three pairs of legs, two antennae, and, in most instances, two pairs of wings.

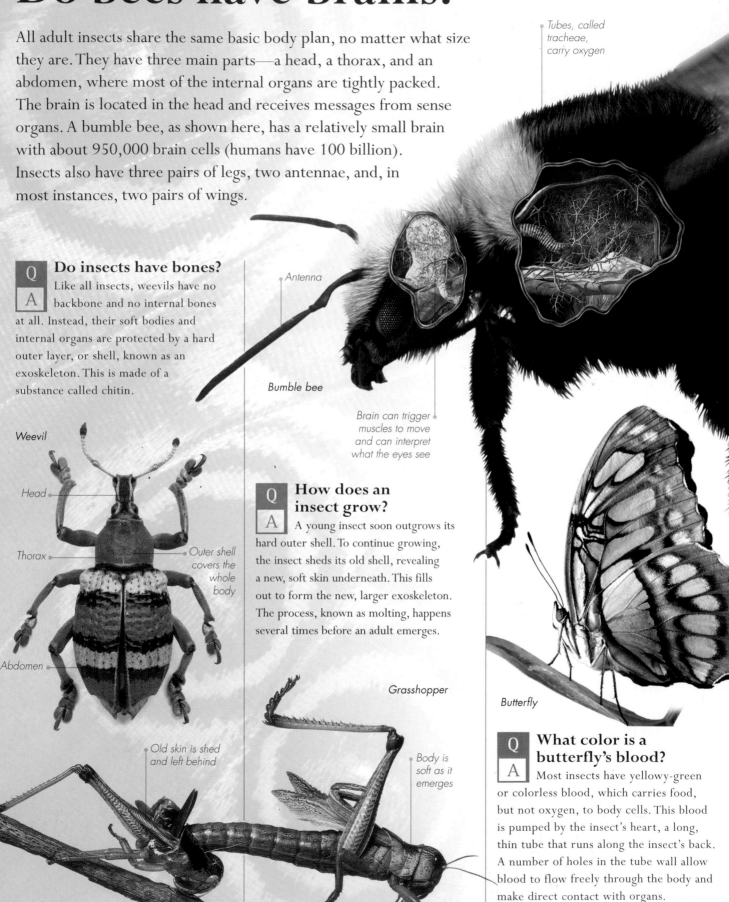

Tubes, called tracheae, carry oxygen

Antenna

Bumble bee

Brain can trigger muscles to move and can interpret what the eyes see

Q A Do insects have bones?
Like all insects, weevils have no backbone and no internal bones at all. Instead, their soft bodies and internal organs are protected by a hard outer layer, or shell, known as an exoskeleton. This is made of a substance called chitin.

Weevil

Head

Thorax

Abdomen

Outer shell covers the whole body

Old skin is shed and left behind

Q A How does an insect grow?
A young insect soon outgrows its hard outer shell. To continue growing, the insect sheds its old shell, revealing a new, soft skin underneath. This fills out to form the new, larger exoskeleton. The process, known as molting, happens several times before an adult emerges.

Grasshopper

Body is soft as it emerges

Butterfly

Q A What color is a butterfly's blood?
Most insects have yellow-green or colorless blood, which carries food, but not oxygen, to body cells. This blood is pumped by the insect's heart, a long, thin tube that runs along the insect's back. A number of holes in the tube wall allow blood to flow freely through the body and make direct contact with organs.

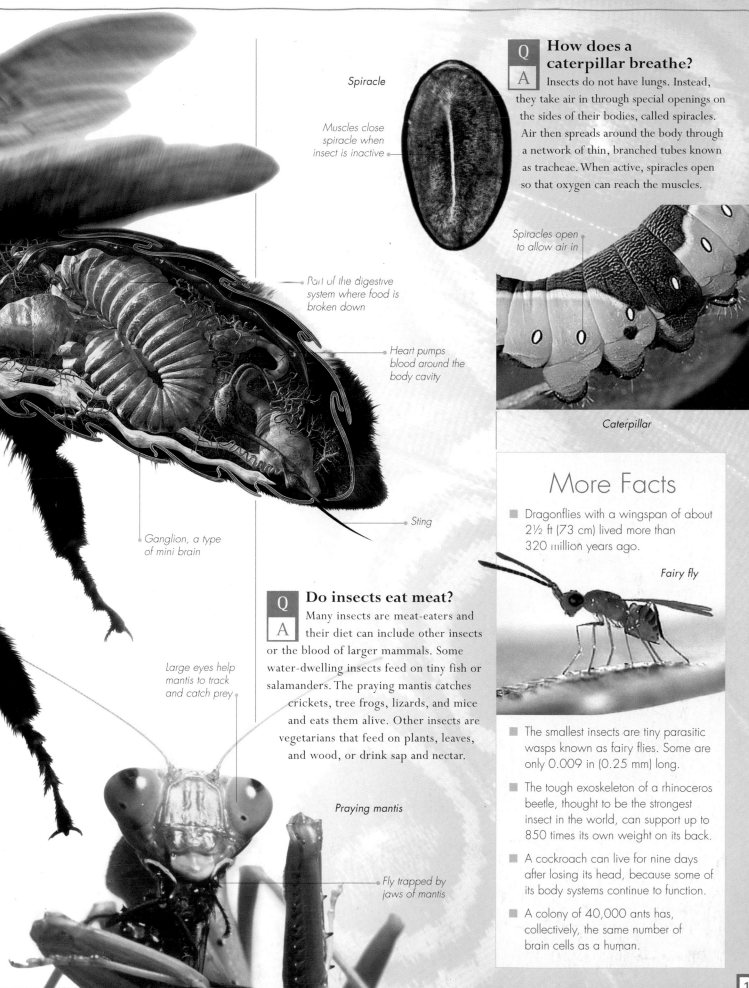

Spiracle

Muscles close
spiracle when
insect is inactive

Part of the digestive
system where food is
broken down

Heart pumps
blood around the
body cavity

Ganglion, a type
of mini brain

Sting

Q A How does a caterpillar breathe?

Insects do not have lungs. Instead, they take air in through special openings on the sides of their bodies, called spiracles. Air then spreads around the body through a network of thin, branched tubes known as tracheae. When active, spiracles open so that oxygen can reach the muscles.

Spiracles open
to allow air in

Caterpillar

Q A Do insects eat meat?

Many insects are meat-eaters and their diet can include other insects or the blood of larger mammals. Some water-dwelling insects feed on tiny fish or salamanders. The praying mantis catches crickets, tree frogs, lizards, and mice and eats them alive. Other insects are vegetarians that feed on plants, leaves, and wood, or drink sap and nectar.

Large eyes help
mantis to track
and catch prey

Praying mantis

Fly trapped by
jaws of mantis

More Facts

- Dragonflies with a wingspan of about 2½ ft (73 cm) lived more than 320 million years ago.

Fairy fly

- The smallest insects are tiny parasitic wasps known as fairy flies. Some are only 0.009 in (0.25 mm) long.

- The tough exoskeleton of a rhinoceros beetle, thought to be the strongest insect in the world, can support up to 850 times its own weight on its back.

- A cockroach can live for nine days after losing its head, because some of its body systems continue to function.

- A colony of 40,000 ants has, collectively, the same number of brain cells as a human.

13

Does every insect have wings?

More than 320 million years ago, insects became the first creatures to take to the air. Flight helped them to escape danger and to find new habitats and has always played an important part in their survival. Most insects have two sets of wings, although some orders also have a few flightless species. Ladybugs, along with many beetles, have two hard forewings that shield and protect the hindwings when not in flight.

Shield bug

Wings form an X-shape on the bug's back

Q A How are the wings of true bugs different?
Most true bugs have two pairs of wings, although some are wingless. On a shield bug, the front wings are thick and tough at the base and very thin at the tips. When the bug is at rest, the wings are held flat over the body and the membranous parts of the wings overlap.

Hard wing case, or elytron

Ladybug

Delicate hindwings are spread for flying

Rigid veins add strength to wings

Lacewing

Q A What are wings made from?
Wings are an extension of an insect's exoskeleton, although the chitin in them is very thin. Some wings have veins that work like the struts of an airplane to give extra strength. Wings can also be covered with scales or fringed with long hairs.

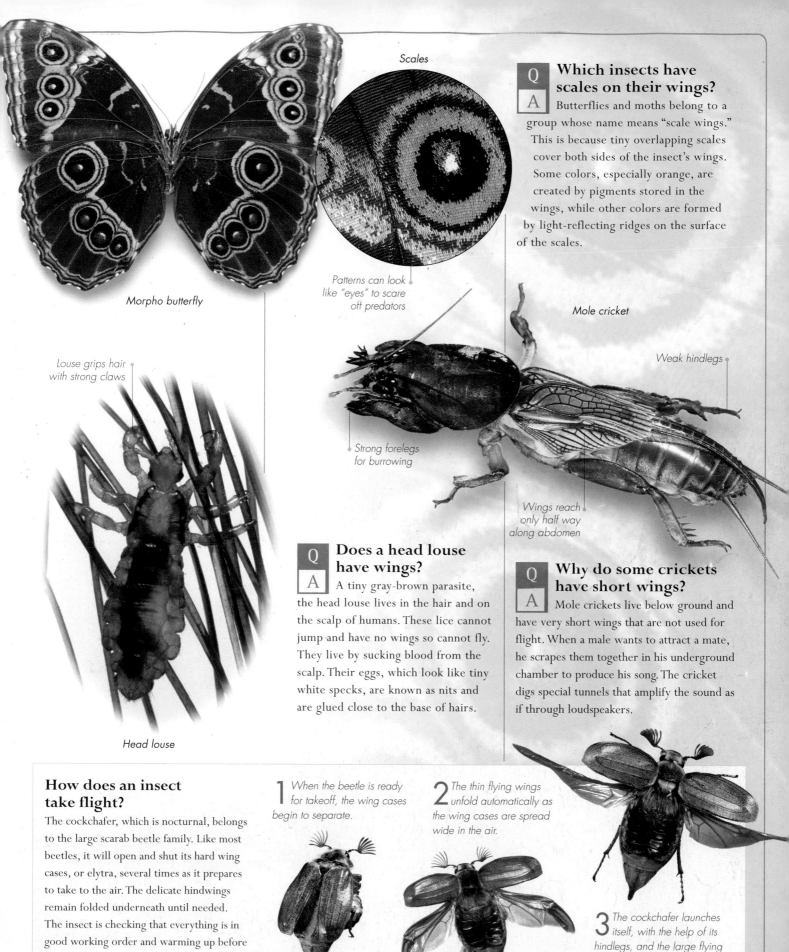

Morpho butterfly

Scales

Patterns can look like "eyes" to scare ott predators

Which insects have scales on their wings?

Q **A** Butterflies and moths belong to a group whose name means "scale wings." This is because tiny overlapping scales cover both sides of the insect's wings. Some colors, especially orange, are created by pigments stored in the wings, while other colors are formed by light-reflecting ridges on the surface of the scales.

Mole cricket

Louse grips hair with strong claws

Weak hindlegs

Strong forelegs for burrowing

Wings reach only half way along abdomen

Does a head louse have wings?

Q **A** A tiny gray-brown parasite, the head louse lives in the hair and on the scalp of humans. These lice cannot jump and have no wings so cannot fly. They live by sucking blood from the scalp. Their eggs, which look like tiny white specks, are known as nits and are glued close to the base of hairs.

Head louse

Why do some crickets have short wings?

Q **A** Mole crickets live below ground and have very short wings that are not used for flight. When a male wants to attract a mate, he scrapes them together in his underground chamber to produce his song. The cricket digs special tunnels that amplify the sound as if through loudspeakers.

How does an insect take flight?

The cockchafer, which is nocturnal, belongs to the large scarab beetle family. Like most beetles, it will open and shut its hard wing cases, or elytra, several times as it prepares to take to the air. The delicate hindwings remain folded underneath until needed. The insect is checking that everything is in good working order and warming up before unfurling its flying wings.

1 _When the beetle is ready for takeoff, the wing cases begin to separate._

2 _The thin flying wings unfold automatically as the wing cases are spread wide in the air._

3 _The cockchafer launches itself, with the help of its hindlegs, and the large flying wings take over._

Can all insects lay eggs?

The life cycle of most insects starts with an egg—usually laid somewhere safe, such as on the underside of a leaf or on the ground. It is the first stage in a long and astonishing process of change, known as metamorphosis. This pattern of growth features four different stages—egg, larva, pupa, and adult insect. The lily beetle lays her shiny red eggs under the leaves of a lily plant. They will go through complete metamorphosis before they become fully formed adult insects.

What is a chrysalis?

When a caterpillar, or larva, emerges from its egg, it enters its second stage of development. It eats and grows, shedding its skin several times until it is ready for the pupal stage. Its final skin hardens into a protective case, called a chrysalis. This is where the pupa becomes a butterfly.

1 When ready, the larva attaches itself to a plant.

Lily beetle and eggs

Larvae hatch from eggs after about 7 days

Adults and larvae feed on lily leaves and sometimes eat the flowers, too

Q A Do any bugs give birth to live young?

Although most insects lay eggs, some give birth to young, known as nymphs. The wingless females of certain species of aphid live together in colonies for much of the year. Each mother can produce as many as 70 live young.

Aphid nymph emerging

Aphid

Q A Which queen is an egg machine?

A queen termite spends her life producing eggs. When she is young, she may only lay 10 or 20 eggs a day, but after a few years the number can rise to more than 1,000 a day. Her body becomes huge and bloated—sometimes too big for her to leave the nesting chamber. Small, blind worker termites look after the eggs and take them away to the nurseries.

Queen termite

2 It then turns into a pupa, which is covered by a case called a chrysalis.

3 The chrysalis hardens in the air and the pupa begins to change shape.

4 After a few days the chrysalis becomes transparent and wings can be seen.

5 After about 10 days, the butterfly emerges and waits for its wings to dry out in the air.

Q A How do earwigs take care of their eggs?

Unlike many insects, the female earwig takes care of her young. She digs a shallow burrow where she lays her eggs, often defending them from intruders. Sometimes, she seals the entrance completely. The mother turns the eggs and rearranges them if they get scattered. After the nymphs have hatched, she feeds them until they leave the nest.

Earwig and eggs

Female licks eggs to keep them clean

Wasp clutches the caterpillar it will use as a host for its young

Ichneumon wasp

Q A Do some wasps lay their eggs on prey?

Some insects lay their eggs in a living host. The female ichneumon wasp, for example, has an egg-laying apparatus, called an ovipositor, which she uses to insert her eggs into a live caterpillar. When they hatch, the larvae start to feed, consuming their victim from within. They pupate on the corpse of the caterpillar and emerge as fully grown adults.

Exoskeleton will be shed as the nymph grows

Bug nymph

Q A Which insect doesn't need a mate?

The females of some species of stick insect reproduce with or without a mate. They can breed parthenogenetically—which means that the young hatch from eggs that have not been fertilized by a male. The young are female clones of their mothers, rather than individuals.

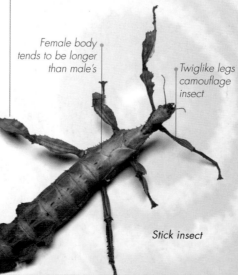

Female body tends to be longer than male's

Twiglike legs camouflage insect

Stick insect

Q A What is incomplete metamorphosis?

Some insects, including true bugs, go through incomplete metamorphosis, which has only three stages—egg, nymph, and adult. The nymphs, which hatch from the eggs, are miniature versions of the adults they will become. The nymphs shed their skins several times as they grow into adult insects.

Is a scorpion an insect?

Many small creatures creep, crawl, or scuttle along the ground and can be mistaken for insects—and scorpions are among them. These creatures belong to a group of animals known as arthropods, which also includes centipedes, spiders, mites, ticks, and crustaceans—as well as insects. They all have several things in common, such as jointed legs, a hard exoskeleton, and segmented bodies. Crustaceans, such as lobsters and crabs, are also arthropods.

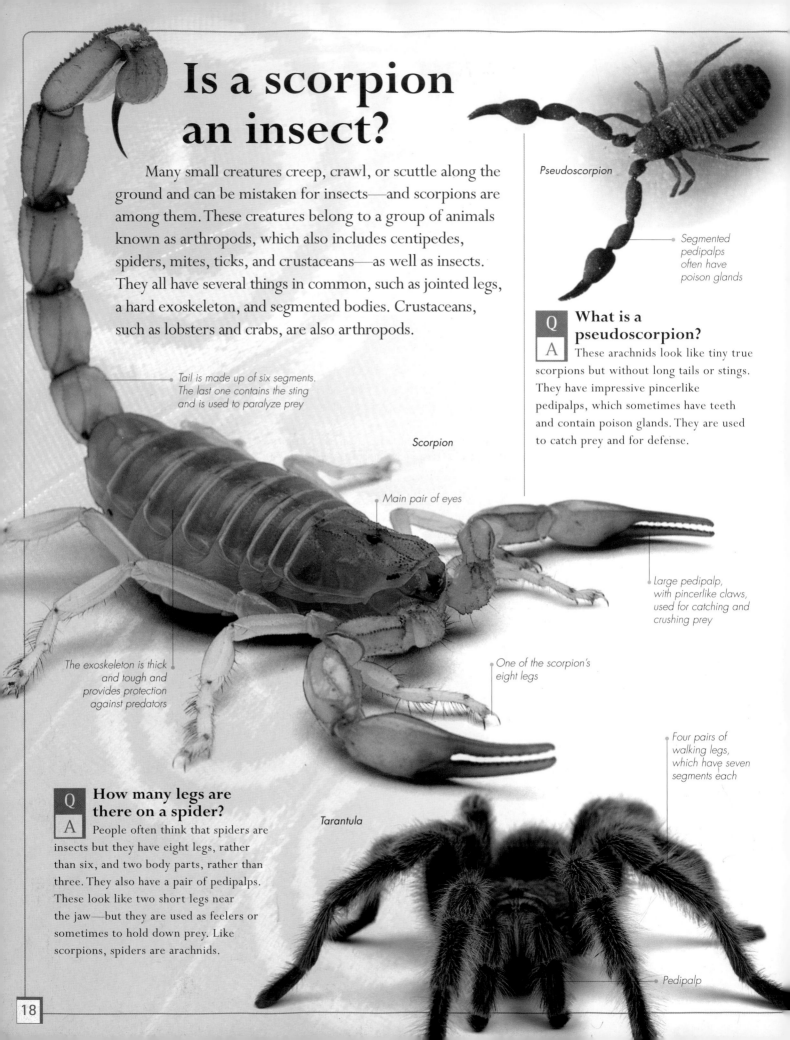

Pseudoscorpion

Segmented pedipalps often have poison glands

Q A **What is a pseudoscorpion?**
These arachnids look like tiny true scorpions but without long tails or stings. They have impressive pincerlike pedipalps, which sometimes have teeth and contain poison glands. They are used to catch prey and for defense.

Tail is made up of six segments. The last one contains the sting and is used to paralyze prey

Scorpion

Main pair of eyes

Large pedipalp, with pincerlike claws, used for catching and crushing prey

The exoskeleton is thick and tough and provides protection against predators

One of the scorpion's eight legs

Four pairs of walking legs, which have seven segments each

Q A **How many legs are there on a spider?**
People often think that spiders are insects but they have eight legs, rather than six, and two body parts, rather than three. They also have a pair of pedipalps. These look like two short legs near the jaw—but they are used as feelers or sometimes to hold down prey. Like scorpions, spiders are arachnids.

Tarantula

Pedipalp

Q A Can a centipede grow new legs?

All centipedes have at least 16 pairs of legs, each attached to a different segment of the body. Young centipedes hatch with several pairs and each time they molt they grow another segment and another new pair of legs. Only a few centipedes live up to their name, which means "one hundred feet."

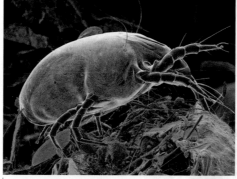

Dust mite

Q A What do dust mites feed on?

Tiny dust mites are less than 0.04 in (1 mm) long and live in mattresses, pillows, carpets, and furniture. They feed on minute particles of organic matter, particularly flakes of human skin. Dust mites are often blamed for conditions such as eczema and asthma, because their droppings can cause an allergic reaction in some people.

More Facts

- Lobsters, which are crustaceans, continue to grow throughout their lives and need to molt, or shed, their hard external skeleton many times.

- Like the flea, the beach flea can jump amazing distances, but it has 10 legs rather than an insect's six.

- After female scorpions give birth, they carry their young on their backs until they are strong enough to fend for themselves.

- The tiny, wingless springtail lives in soil and leaf litter. They were once classified as insects, but scientists have now placed them in a different group.

Springtail

Pair of segmented antennae, about one-third length of body

Centipede

A pair of legs is attached to each body segment

Sheep tick

The last pair of legs is the longest

Woodlouse

Q A Where do woodlice like to live?

These prehistoric-looking creatures are crustaceans and, unlike insects, they breathe through gills. They need moisture, so generally live in damp, dark places—under rocks or logs. Woodlice have flexible, segmented bodies that enable them to curl up when threatened. They are the only crustaceans to live and breed on land.

Short, translucent legs

Q A Are ticks the same as fleas?

Ticks are external parasites, which live by feeding on the blood of other animals, in the same way as fleas. But ticks are not insects, they are arachnids and close relatives of mites. They have four pairs of legs and thin, flat bodies that become swollen with blood after they have feasted on a host animal.

Habitats and homes

Are there insects in deserts?

From snow-covered mountains to tropical rain forests and from hot, sandy deserts to dark, dank caves, insects have adapted to almost every habitat on the planet. This ability to live anywhere is one of the main reasons for their successful survival. On a foggy morning, one desert beetle waits patiently on top of a sand dune to get a drink. The moisture in the air eventually turns to water on the insect's hard shell and runs down its back into its mouth.

Darkling beetle

Drops of water form on the insect's body

Q **Are there any insects in Antarctica?**

A A small, wingless fly—the Antarctic midge—is the largest animal to live permanently on land on the world's coldest continent. The midges are found within penguin colonies, where they feed on algae and bird droppings. The midge larvae spend the winter encased in ice.

Body is about ½ in (1 cm) long

Antarctic midges

Q **How do ladybugs survive the cold?**

A Ladybugs often hibernate in large groups—sometimes in the thousands. They usually gather in a sheltered spot among thick vegetation, leaf litter, or under the bark of a tree, and stay inactive until the spring. Sometimes they settle in sheds or old buildings—and two-spot ladybugs even hibernate inside houses. Ladybugs usually return to the same place each winter.

Hibernating ladybugs

Which weevils live in woodlands?

Q / **A** Acorn weevils are beetles that live in oak trees. They have long snouts, which can be almost as long as their bodies. Super-sharp jaws help them to drill into acorns and eat the soft food inside. Females lay their eggs inside acorns and seal them tightly with a dropping.

Long jointed legs with feet for gripping

Acorn weevil

Extended snout, known as rostrum, with mouth at the end

Which insects thrive in the rain forest?

Q / **A** Tropical rain forests are home to a huge number of insects. The fulgorid bug, which can grow up to 3 in (7.5 cm) long, is one of the largest plant-hoppers. Its strange extended mouthparts are adapted for sucking up plant sap. If alarmed while feeding, the bugs will flick open their wings to reveal warning eyespots.

Large snout

Colorful wings with bright eyespots

Fulgorid bug

More Facts

- One species of midge spends its entire life in the Yala Glacier in the Himalayas of Asia, at nearly 18,000 ft (5,500 m).

- Nocturnal and flightless, the Weta, found only in New Zealand, lives in a variety of environments, including alpine forests, grasslands, and caves.

Weta

- The larvae of one species of scarab beetle, found in the Galapagos Islands, live in the eggs of green sea turtles.

- Some tropical moths drink the tears of horses and elephants for their salt content.

- Witchetty grubs, found mainly in central Australia, are the wood-eating larvae of various types of moths.

Woolly bear caterpillar

Are there any insects in the Arctic?

Q / **A** The Arctic woolly bear caterpillar freezes solid in subzero temperatures for the 10 months of winter. Its vital organs are protected by a natural antifreeze called glycerol. After thawing out, the caterpillar grows a little during the brief summer, before freezing again. It can take up to 14 years to become an adult moth.

Brine flies

Huge clouds of brine flies provide food for shore birds

Can flies survive in salt water?

Q / **A** Brine flies have adapted to some unusual habitats, including saltwater lakes. During the summer, females lay eggs on the surface of the water. When these hatch, the larvae feed on algae along the shore. As adult flies emerge from their pupae, they each surround themselves in an air bubble and float to the surface.

What is a social insect?

Some insects live together permanently in large groups and are called social, while others are solitary. Social insects live in colonies that may have a few dozen members or hundreds of thousands. They work as a team to build a nest, find food, and care for the young. Ants, termites, and some bees and wasps are highly social, and their colonies are well structured and efficient. Honey bees work in harmony, keeping their hives clean and storing food for the winter.

Who is the queen bee?

There is one fertile female in each colony, known as the queen, and she lays all the eggs. Although she is the queen, she works nonstop, spending her whole life laying eggs—up to 2,000 a day.

1 *The queen is the largest member of the colony. Her reign lasts two to three years, until another egg-layer takes over.*

2 *The drones are the male members of the hive. Their function is to mate with the queen, after which they die.*

3 *There are usually thousands of workers— sterile females who feed and tend the queen and the young.*

Six-sided cells with larvae

Cells with larvae are left open so that workers can feed them

The faster the bees dance, the closer the food

Waggle dance

Q | A Where does the queen lay her eggs?

The queen lays an egg in each cell on the honeycomb. This is where it will hatch into a larva and then pupate, before turning into an adult bee. The young are known as the brood, and the nursery area is the brood comb. Larvae are fed with royal jelly, made by the workers, and later with honey and pollen. A larva fed on royal jelly alone will turn into a new queen.

Q | A How do bees find food?

Worker bees gather nectar and pollen for the rest of the colony. When they have found a good supply, they perfom a special "waggle" dance on the honeycomb to communicate the exact location of the food to the others.

Workers produce wax and mold it into honeycomb

Worker honey bees on honeycomb

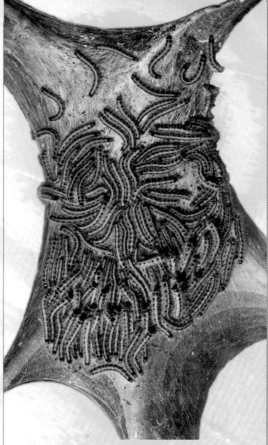

Eastern tent caterpillars

Flying ants perform airborne mating ritual once a year

Flying ants

Q / A — Who starts an ant colony?

A new ant colony is started by a young queen, after she has mated in flight. Her male mate dies soon after, his job completed. The queen lands and finds a suitable place to start a new nest, sheds her wings, and begins to lay eggs. The new colony is born.

Q / A — Are caterpillars social?

No, they are not considered social. However, Eastern tent caterpillars hatch from clusters of eggs laid on twigs or branches. The caterpillars then stay and spin a silken tent—often in a fork in the tree— and spend this stage of their life feeding and growing together. The group breaks up when the caterpillars are ready to pupate.

Q / A — How do ants keep in touch?

Like most social insects, ants need to communicate with each other. Since worker ants have small eyes, they have to rely on their sense of touch and smell. To achieve this, they use their long and highly sensitive antennae, which contain both touch and smell organs. Each ant colony has a unique odor, so members recognize each other and sniff out intruders.

Flexible antennae keep ants in touch

Ants touching antennae

Which insects are skillful builders?

Nests come in all shapes and sizes, but the largest and most elaborate structures are usually made by social insects. Many ants and termites build complex warrens of tunnels, chambers, and galleries deep underground. Solitary insects make do with simple nests—often just a small burrow in the soil or a hole in a tree. Migrant army ants turn themselves into temporary living nests, known as bivouacs, as they swarm through the jungle.

Holes at top for ventilation

Australian termite mound

Towers can reach 20 ft (6 m) high

Army ant bivouac

Q A How do termites build their mounds?

Small, blind worker termites construct huge towers above their nests using tiny pieces of soil mixed with saliva or dung. The underground nests can house up to five million well-organized termites. Air channels from the nest to the tower disperse warm, moist air given off by the termites.

Q A Which insects live in dead wood?

Many species of wood-boring insect make their homes in decaying tree stumps and logs. Bess beetles chew their way through the dead wood, making tunnels and chambers as they go. The wood provides the beetles with both food and shelter and also helps to recycle the dead wood.

Bess beetle

More Facts

- One type of rove beetle makes its burrow by the sea with such narrow openings that the air pressure inside keeps the tide out.

- Tropical ants make nests from leaves, sticking the edges together with silk from their live larvae.

- Termite nests include nursery chambers, a royal cell for the queen, and access points to water.

- Web spinners make silken webs and tunnels under stones, logs, and in the soil. They live in small communities of a dozen or so individuals.

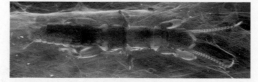

Web spinner

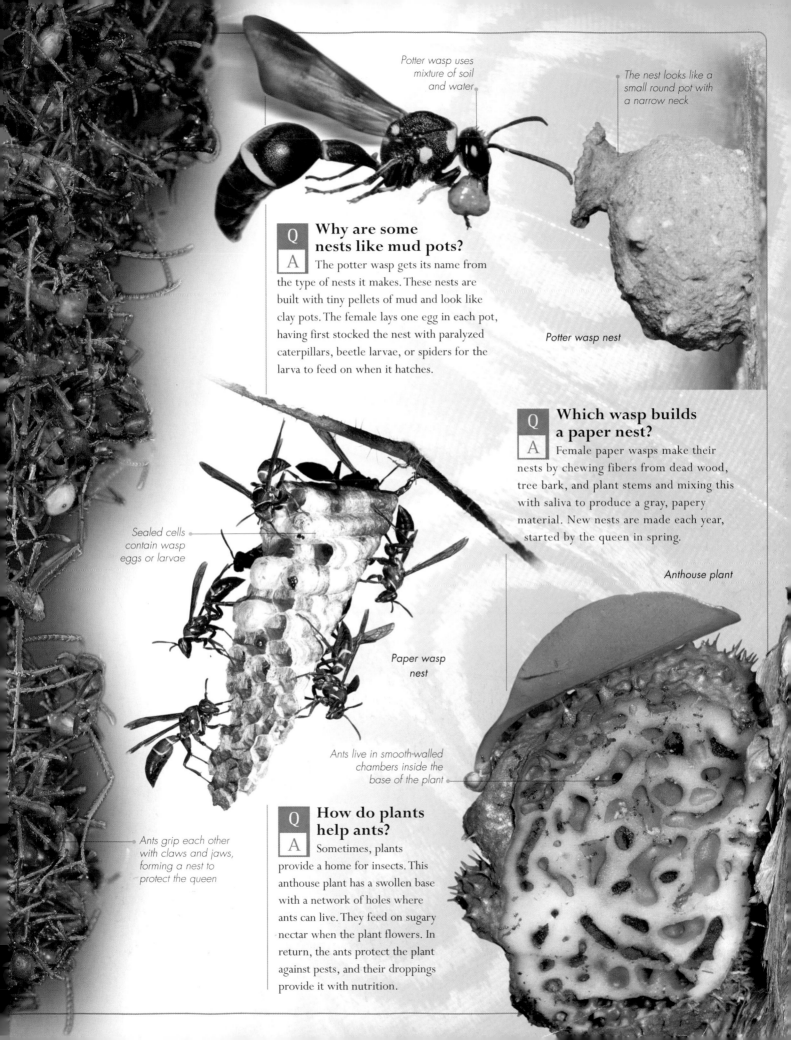

Potter wasp uses mixture of soil and water

The nest looks like a small round pot with a narrow neck

Q&A Why are some nests like mud pots?

The potter wasp gets its name from the type of nests it makes. These nests are built with tiny pellets of mud and look like clay pots. The female lays one egg in each pot, having first stocked the nest with paralyzed caterpillars, beetle larvae, or spiders for the larva to feed on when it hatches.

Potter wasp nest

Q&A Which wasp builds a paper nest?

Female paper wasps make their nests by chewing fibers from dead wood, tree bark, and plant stems and mixing this with saliva to produce a gray, papery material. New nests are made each year, started by the queen in spring.

Anthouse plant

Sealed cells contain wasp eggs or larvae

Paper wasp nest

Ants live in smooth-walled chambers inside the base of the plant

Ants grip each other with claws and jaws, forming a nest to protect the queen

Q&A How do plants help ants?

Sometimes, plants provide a home for insects. This anthouse plant has a swollen base with a network of holes where ants can live. They feed on sugary nectar when the plant flowers. In return, the ants protect the plant against pests, and their droppings provide it with nutrition.

Can bugs live underwater?

Although insects evolved on land, many have adapted to live in the fresh water of ponds, lakes, and rivers. Some spend their entire life cycles in water. Others live there only as larvae or nymphs—feeding on the rich food supplies— and leave when they become winged adults. To survive in their watery world, insects have developed ways to breathe underwater. The water scorpion, for example, takes in air through a long, thin tube at the tip of its body.

Q A How do insects breathe underwater?
Many aquatic insects come to the surface for oxygen. Others, such as the great diving beetle, use different methods. While they are at the larva stage, they draw air from the surface through tubes on their tails. When they are adults, they trap a bubble of air under their front wings, and breathe from it as they swim after prey.

Powerful front legs for seizing prey

Great diving beetle

Long hind legs are used for swimming

Water scorpion

Mayfly nymph

Gills

Hollow tube is pushed through the water's surface to take in air

Q A Do some insects have gills?
Most nymphs that live underwater have external gills, so they can extract air from the water like fish. The damselfly nymph has three gills at the tip of its body, while the mayfly nymph breathes through feathery gills along the sides of its abdomen.

28

Backswimmer

Long back legs are used for swimming; front and middle legs catch prey

More Facts

- Some aquatic beetle larvae tap into plants and breathe oxygen through their stems.

- Sea skaters, or ocean striders, are the only marine insects. They feed on anything that floats to the surface, such as dead jellyfish or fish eggs.

- Some caddisfly larvae spin cocoons and stick small stones, pieces of plant, and sand onto them for camouflage and protection underwater.

- The giant water bug is one of the biggest true bugs. It measures up to 4½ in (11.5 cm) long and has a wingspan of 8½ in (21.6 cm).

Some females lay eggs on the backs of their mates, who guard them until they hatch

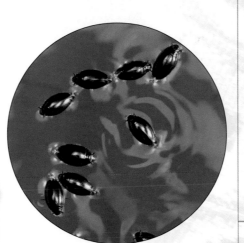

Hatched egg

Giant water bug and eggs

Q A Why are long hairy legs helpful?

Water measurers live on top of the water. They walk slowly over the surface with the help of special water-repelling hairs on their long legs. The "repulsive" force between the water and these hairs is enough to support the weight of the insects on the surface of the water.

Whirligig beetles

Q A Which beetle swims in circles?

If they sense danger, whirligig beetles whirl around in great numbers like spinning tops on the surface of quiet lakes, ponds, and slow-flowing streams to baffle predators. They are smooth and streamlined and zip around by using their short middle and back legs like paddles.

Hairs grow on the undersides of the insect's long legs

Water measurer

Q A How did backswimmers get their name?

These small, oval bugs swim upside down on their backs, paddling vigorously with their long, hair-fringed back legs. Backswimmers collect oxygen from the surface and use it to breathe and float underwater. They hunt for insects, tadpoles, and small fish just below the surface of the water in ponds and ditches.

Breathing tube extends from last segment of abdomen

Larvae hang motionless under the water's surface

Mosquito larvae

Q A Who hangs around on the water's surface?

Mosquitoes often lay their eggs on the surface of the water—either singly or in clusters of between 30 and 300, known as rafts. Within a week they hatch into larvae that live in the water and that breathe through air tubes poked through the surface. The larvae eat organic matter from the water and sometimes feed on other species of mosquito larvae.

Senses

How do insects see the world?

Like most animals, insects use their sight to help them make sense of their surroundings. But their large compound eyes work in a different way from human eyes. Rather than having a single lens in each eye, an insect may have hundreds or thousands of "mini eyes" that create a mosaic-type image. Although insects are quick to spot movement, they are generally unable to make out fine details. Aerial predators, like this horse fly, have larger eyes and sharper vision than many other insects.

Q A Who has simple eyes?

Most nymphs and adult insects have three simple eyes as well as two compound eyes. Compound eyes have thousands of tiny, six-sided lenses that fit together like a honeycomb. Simple eyes have just one lens and can only tell the difference between light and dark. Some immature insects, such as caterpillars, only have simple eyes. The praying mantis has three simple eyes and two compound eyes.

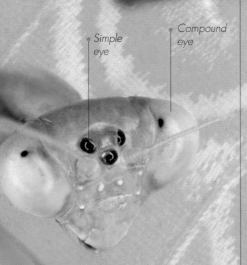

Simple eye

Compound eye

Praying mantis

Q A Do insects see in color?

Many insects with compound eyes have color vision, but very few—aside from butterflies—can see red. They are better at seeing shades of blue. Butterflies can also detect ultraviolet light, which is invisible to the human eye. This allows them to see special patterns on the petals of flowers, which guide them to the nectar they feed on.

Flower appears yellow

Dandelion as seen with human eyes

Nectar guide attracts insect

Dandelion photographed in ultraviolet

Compound eyes of horse fly

Eyes cover most of
head so fly has wide
field of vision

*Spicebush swallowtail
caterpillar*

False eyes

Q A How many eyes does a caterpillar have?

Caterpillars can have five, six, or seven small, simple eyes along each side of the head. But some caterpillars have false eyes, known as pseudo-eyes, which cannot see at all. They are just decoys on the surface of the body that make the caterpillar look more fierce and scare away hungry predators.

Q A Can insects see in the dark?

Insects that are active at night have eyes that help them make the most of available light in the dimmest conditions. Some night-flying moths have evolved special structures in the eyes that stop light from reflecting and escaping. Others can also see in color and can find flowers in dim light.

Specially adapted
compound eyes

Striped hawkmoth

More Facts

■ Dragonflies have excellent vision, with more than 10,000 lenses in each compound eye.

Eyes cover most of head

Dragonfly

■ The eyes of a praying mantis change color, depending on the angle of the light. They appear light green or tan in bright light and brown in the dark.

■ Some water surface-living beetles have eyes that can see above and below the water.

■ Flies and mosquitoes are very nearsighted and can only see a short distance in front of them.

Tiny hairs at
junctions of
lenses

Each
compound
eye has
6,900 lenses

Q A Which insect has hairy eyes?

Honey bees have large compound eyes, which help them to locate good sources of nectar. The surface of each eye is covered with long thin hairs, which help the bees to gauge the speed and direction of the wind as they fly. Sometimes bees have to cover great distances to collect the nectar and take it back to the hive.

Honey bee

What do feelers feel?

Antennae are often called "feelers" because insects use them to feel their way around. These multipurpose sense organs, which vary between species, help insects to locate mates, find food, and secure places to lay their eggs. Many are covered with tiny hairs that can detect movement and vibrations in the air. Antennae come in a range of shapes and sizes—this male moth has spectacular plumed antennae that it uses to pick up the special scent, or pheromone, of females.

Long, fine antenna

Cave cricket

Q A Which insects have long antennae?

Wingless cave crickets are found in damp, dark places like cellars, basements, and caves. Some species have very limited or no sight and spend their whole lives in darkness. Their extremely long antennae help them to sense their surroundings, find their way around, and detect predators.

Male atlas moth

Fine hairs on the antenna are called sensilla

Hairs can detect scent of female up to 2¾ miles (4.5 km) away

Q A How do dung beetles find dung?

Each dung beetle species has its own favorite type of animal dung, and their antennae can pick up the smell from more than 10 miles (16 km) away. They fly to find it, and when they do they roll it into a ball and lay their eggs in it. Extensions on the ends of their antennae are covered with sensilla.

Mosquito

Q A Who has feathery antennae?

Male mosquitoes have ornate and elaborate antennae that look like tiny feather dusters. These antennae are extremely sensitive and can pick up the vibration of a distant female mosquito's wings beating in the air. Female mosquitoes have shorter and simpler antennae.

Ball of dung

Dung beetle

More Facts

■ Some lacewings use tiny "ears" at the base of their forewings to detect ultrasonic signals from predatory bats.

■ Female crickets can taste with the ovipositor (egg-laying organ) at the end of their body.

■ The Indian moon moth has a great sense of smell and can detect a mate from more than 6 miles (9.5 km) away.

Jewel beetle

Infrared sense organ located under body

■ Some jewel beetles lay eggs in burned wood. Their infrared detection organs can sense a suitable habitat from up to 50 miles (80 km) away.

■ Longhorn beetles' antennae can be four times the length of their bodies.

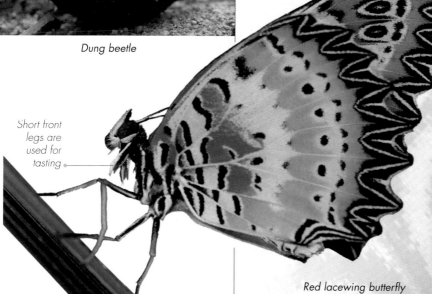
Short front legs are used for tasting

Red lacewing butterfly

Caterpillar

Long hairs are sensitive to touch

Q A Can a butterfly really taste with its feet?

Some butterflies have tiny taste sensors on their short front legs. When they are looking for a plant on which to lay their eggs, they use their front legs to taste the plant's leaves. By doing this, they make sure that their caterpillars will have a good supply of suitable food to eat when they hatch. A butterfly's long, strawlike mouth is for drinking nectar only and does not have any taste sensors.

Q A How do caterpillars sense danger?

The bodies of some caterpillars are covered with fine hairs or bristles that are known as setae. They are attached to nerve cells and can detect touch and vibration, sending messages to the brain when danger approaches. Setae can sting and may also be used for defensive purposes.

How do insects communicate?

Insects have a sophisticated range of ways to communicate with each other—from touching to flashing signals and singing. Social insects in particular need ways to organize their large colonies. Some produce special chemicals called pheromones. Leafcutter ants use these chemicals to lay a trail back to the nest when a good source of leaves has been found. Other members of the colony then pick up the scent and follow it, carrying the leaves back to the nest.

Honey bees secrete pheromones from glands in their abdomen

Honey bee

Q&A

How do insects use pheromones?

Pheromones are like chemical signals that trigger a particular response in other insects—usually members of the same species. They are often carried in the air, but are sometimes laid on the ground. Many insects use pheromones to recognize each other or to find a mate. Honey bees use them to find food, protect eggs, and raise the alarm.

Leafcutter ants

Leaf fragments can be 20 times heavier than the weight of the ant

Fireflies

Males use their green flashes to attract mates

Q&A

Why do some bugs flash?

Each species of firefly has a precise pattern of flashing with a unique time sequence. When a female recognizes a male, she answers with a corresponding flash. Some predatory females are able to imitate the signals of other species, and lure the males to them to eat.

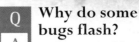

36

More Facts

- Ants play "follow the leader" when on the move by tapping the hind legs of the ant in front with their antennae.

- The hermit beetle releases a chemical that smells like leather to attract a mate.

Large copper butterfly caterpillar

- Large copper butterfly caterpillars produce a chemical that attracts ants. The ants then protect the caterpillars as if they were their own larvae.

- During courtship, some male butterflies produce scents from modified scales on their wings to increase their chances of success.

Larger back leg produces a song when rubbed over folded wing

Short-horned grasshopper

Q A How do grasshoppers sing in summer?
The familiar sound of grasshoppers in summer comes from an all-male choir, each male singing a unique song in an attempt to attract a mate. Short-horned grasshoppers rub a row of pegs on their back legs over the edge of their folded wings. Crickets have a similar kind of mechanism, but it is on the forewings.

Q A Who offers his mate a meal?
Male scorpion flies produce special pheromones from glands in their abdomens when they are ready to attract females. Sometimes they also offer a meal of insect prey or a ball of regurgitated saliva. The females feed on this as mating takes place. Males often steal this prey from each another—sometimes by pretending to be females.

Scorpion flies

Ants use the leaves to grow fungus to feed to their larvae

Treehopper

Sensors throughout the body can pick up vibrations

Q A How do treehoppers warn of danger?
Many species of treehopper are social, forming large groups that live together in the same tree. When danger approaches, some species warn each other by vibrating, which sends a signal through the twigs and branches of the tree. Treehoppers also produce a complex set of sounds to entice a mate.

Where do insects go in winter?

Surviving winter can be a challenge for many creatures. Insects are cold-blooded, so most of them need to absorb heat from their surroundings, since they are unable to keep themselves warm. To beat the cold, they have various strategies such as hibernation or migration. Many immature insects spend the winter in a sheltered spot—as eggs, larvae, or pupae. The brimstone butterfly hibernates during the coldest months to emerge again in spring.

This butterfly can survive an early frost, despite leaving its hibernation spot among evergreens

Brimstone butterfly

More Facts

- The mourning cloak butterfly spends the winter in tree holes or other shelters and is usually one of the first butterflies to be seen in spring.

- The winter moth is one of several moths that can fly even when temperatures drop to freezing.

- The queen bumble bee spends winter asleep in her underground burrow.

- Many aquatic insects are active all winter, since water does not lose its heat as quickly as the land.

- The winter gnat is still active on mild winter nights when predators, like house martins and swallows, have migrated south.

Winter gnat

Harvester ants

Ants carry buds back to their nest

Who stays safe underground?

Q A June bugs have a one-year life cycle. When larvae emerge from eggs, they spend all summer feeding, and then dig burrows where they spend the winter months. In the spring, they start feeding again and emerge in June to mate, lay their eggs, and start the cycle over again.

Legs with stout spines are good for digging deep underground

June bug

How do ants prepare for winter?

Q A Most ants eat large amounts of food in the fall so they don't need to eat during the winter. But harvester ants collect vast quantities of buds, which they stockpile in their deep underground nests to see them through the coldest months. They store the buds in special granaries, where they won't rot or start to germinate.

Pupa is contained in protective cocoon

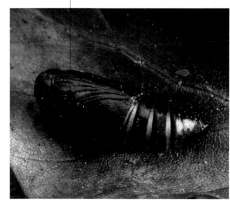

Moth pupa

Queen hibernates before emerging in spring to start a new nest

Hornet

Why do butterflies head south?

Q A Some insects avoid the coldest months of the year by migrating to warmer parts of the world. Each year, huge swarms of monarch butterflies fly from Canada to Mexico in the fall to escape the harsh northern winter. They fly more than 3,000 miles (4,800 km), feeding on milkweed plants all the way.

How does a pupa survive winter?

Q A Many moths and butterflies spend the winter as pupae, sheltered from the cold by a hard, protective coating. Moth pupae usually have an additional, outer covering known as a cocoon, which the caterpillar makes just before it enters the pupa stage. Cocoons can be found in the soil or under the ground, underneath tree bark or suspended from branches or twigs.

How does a hornet avoid the cold?

Q A Hornets live together in nests, which are started each spring. The nests last for less than a year, since the members start to die off as winter approaches. Only the fertilized females—or queens—will live to see the following year. They find a sheltered spot under the ground or in a tree to escape the coldest weather.

Bright colors warn birds that monarchs are poisonous

Monarch butterflies

Survival Skills

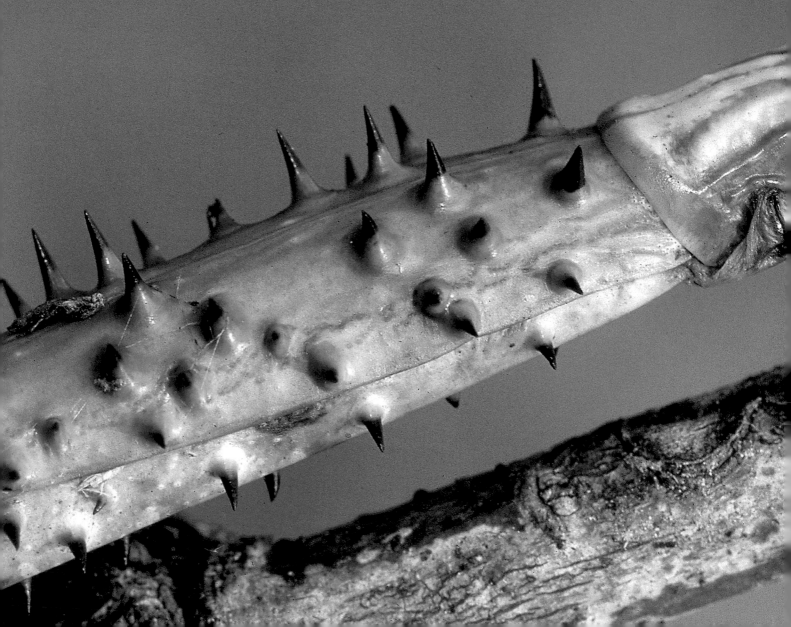

Clusters of
stinging
hairs

Cup moth caterpillar

How does a bug strike back?

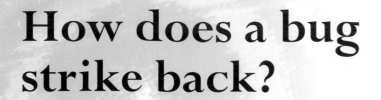

Insects are generally small, but still have to survive in a large and dangerous world. They are hunted by most animals, including birds, amphibians, reptiles, and small mammals. But some of their fiercest predators are fellow insects. Not surprisingly, they have developed an impressive array of survival skills to cope with attack—from toxic froth to sharp spines and killer stings. This longhorn beetle has powerful jaws that it uses to strike back and defend itself.

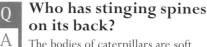

Q A **Who has stinging spines on its back?**
The bodies of caterpillars are soft and vulnerable to hungry predators, such as birds. Some caterpillars protect themselves with a thick coat of poisonous hairs.

The cup moth caterpillar displays small clusters of stinging spines at each end of its body. These are raised when the caterpillar is disturbed, but drawn back inside tubes when it is at rest.

*Rows of sharp teeth
line the jaws*

Antenna

*Compound eye can
detect the slightest
movement of a
potential predator*

*Close-up view of
longhorn beetle*

Curved spine

Powerful, toothed jaws are used to hold victims

Long stinger at tip of abdomen

Bulldog ant

Froth comes from gland openings in grasshopper's thorax

Q A Who produces foul-smelling froth?

Some insects have more than one way to defend themselves. This African grasshopper displays warning colors, but it also emits a foul-smelling and toxic froth from its body when threatened. Like other insects that use this type of defense, the grasshopper gets its poison from the plants it eats.

African grasshopper

Q A Which insect can give you blisters?

Adult blister beetles produce an oily fluid, called cantharidin, to deter their predators. It is a toxic chemical that can cause painful blisters and swellings if it comes in contact with human skin. Blister beetles can also be fatal to animals when swallowed along with their hay feed.

Blister beetle

Stink bug

Bright-striped markings act as warning

Q A Which bugs create a stink?

Shield bugs are true bugs and are often known as stink bugs, because of the terrible smell they can make. They have special glands in their thoraxes, between the first and second pairs of legs, that produce a nasty-smelling liquid when danger looms.

Toxic fluids are secreted from the joints of the legs

Q A Are there ants with killer stings?

There are many species of stinging ant, including fire ants, but bulldog ants are among the largest and most ferocious of all. Their stingers are loaded with venom, which is injected into their victims—often several times. They guard their nests fiercely and attack anything that comes near, grasping their victims with their jaws before stinging them.

More Facts

■ The bombardier beetle squirts a hot, toxic gas out of an opening in the tip of its abdomen with a large "pop"— and remarkable accuracy.

Bombardier beetle

■ The hickory horned devil caterpillar has five pairs of horns on its thorax and spikes on its abdomen to deter predators.

■ The hawkmoth caterpillar from Brazil inflates its thorax and rears its head to fool predators into thinking that it's a small poisonous snake.

Who jumps away from danger?

Attack can be an excellent form of defense, but it is sometimes safer to escape. Many insects are highly skilled at sensing danger and can jump, leap, or hop out of harm's way in less than the blink of an eye. Some insects, such as locusts and grasshoppers, have strong, muscular back legs that allow them to leap great distances. Others can hurl themselves high in the air without even using their legs.

Toughened forewings display camouflage coloring as the insect jumps out of danger

Desert locust

Strong hind legs are good for jumping and kicking

Wings open wide to propel insect farther

Q A Which bugs are amazing athletes?

Froghoppers include some of the most athletic jumpers in the insect world. They flex bowlike structures between their hind legs and wings and release the energy in a catapultlike action. They can leap 100 times their body length to escape attack.

Froghopper

Mechanism on underside of body launches beetle

Q A How does a beetle get off its back?

If click beetles are turned over by predators, they sometimes get stuck. However, they can right themselves using a special mechanism under their bodies. They arch their backs and jackknife high in the air—up to 12 in (30 cm)—making a loud "click." It often takes several attempts before they land on their feet.

Wings are spread wide open

Click beetle

More Facts

- Cheese skippers, larvae of the cheese fly, grasp their tails in their mouths and then release them to launch themselves into the air.

- The devil's coach horse beetle can curve its abdomen up in the air to look like a scorpion and scare predators into running away.

Devil's coach horse beetle

- Flea beetles are small, jumping insects that belong to the leaf beetle family. They have thick, strong hind legs and can leap out of danger, using the "springs" in their knees.

- Fleas use their hind legs to jump onto hosts as they come close. They can jump 200 times their body length.

Extra long antenna

American cockroach

Sensitive cerci sit at rear end of insect

Jaws snap shut at speeds of up to 145 mph (233 km/h)

Q A How does a cockroach sense danger?

Cockroaches are active at night but hide in cracks and crevices during the day. They have two tiny organs—known as cerci—that help them to sense danger. These cerci are covered with tiny hairs and look a little like small antennae, except that they are at the wrong end of the body. When the cerci pick up any disturbance in the air, the cockroach runs in the opposite direction and hides.

Trapjaw ant

Q A Which insect uses its jaws to get away?

The trapjaw ant gets its name from the incredible speed at which its jaws spring shut around its prey. But the insect has another skill—it uses its fearsome jaws to escape from danger. It strikes them against the ground with such force that it catapults the ant into the air and away from predators, such as lizards.

Muscles in thorax move wings up and down

Q A Why are flies always one jump ahead?

Flies are very quick to sense danger—their brains processing the information with lightning speed. They respond in a split second, calculating the exact location of the threat and positioning their legs accordingly for a quick getaway. They kick off into the air, like skilled gymnasts, and then fly away in the safest direction.

Wings flap about 200 times per second

Fly

Large compound eyes have an almost 360-degree field of vision

When is a leaf not a leaf?

Some insects don't need to rely on powerful jaws or muscular legs to get them out of trouble. Instead, they use their camouflage coloring to blend in with the environment and take on the appearance of a leaf, a twig, or even part of a flower. This walking leaf insect looks exactly like a leaf and is perfectly matched to its background. Another strategy is to mimic the markings of poisonous or stinging insects that are less likely to be attacked. Whatever the method, the goal is always to stay out of trouble.

Covering of sand helps conceal bug waiting for prey

Assassin bug nymph

Q A Who covers up?
Assassin bug nymphs often disguise themselves with a cover of dust, sand, and soil. They sometimes add the empty shells of prey on top, too. This helps them to avoid predators, such as spiders and centipedes.

Wings veined in the same way as a leaf

Walking leaf insect

Q A Why do some insects mimic wasps?
Harmless insects sometimes protect themselves from predators by pretending to be dangerous. Robber flies, hover flies, moths, and longhorn beetles are just some of the species that mimic wasps and bees. Some even imitate their movements and the sounds that they make.

Hind wing with white patch

Borneo longhorn beetle

Tarantula hawk wasp

Front wing with white patch

Which bugs have leaves on their legs?

Q A Leaf-footed bugs belong to the true bug family and feed on plants. They get their name from the large, flat flaps on the lower parts of their long back legs. These protect the insect from birds by encouraging them to peck the back leg instead of the head. Nymphs develop these flaps as they near adulthood.

Orchid mantis

Can an insect look like a flower?

Q A The delicately colored orchid mantis thrives in tropical rain forests. It blends in perfectly with the exotic orchid flower where it quietly waits for its prey. The mantis has four walking legs, which can look like leaves or petals. With each succcessive molt, young nymphs grow and take on the colors of their surroundings.

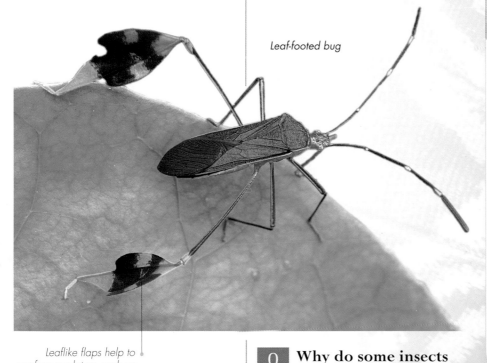

Leaf-footed bug

Leaflike flaps help to confuse predators, such as birds and spiders

Which caterpillar looks like a bird dropping?

The swallowtail butterfly lays her eggs on the milk parsley plant. When they first hatch, the caterpillars resemble bird droppings, making them unappealing to predators. As they grow, they change color so that they blend into the leaves they live on.

1 *Young caterpillars look like bird droppings, which prevents them from being eaten.*

2 *After two molts, the caterpillars develop green bodies that are camouflaged against the leaves.*

Why do some insects look like sticks?

Q A Stick insects are almost impossible to see as they sit among the trees, looking just like twigs. This jumping stick is, in fact, a type of grasshopper that has evolved the same method of camouflage. They are so named because they can jump 35 in (90 cm) into the air.

Prominent eyes

Long, slender legs are segmented, with spines and ridges

Jumping stick

3 *Large yellow swallowtail has safely developed into an adult buterfly.*

How long is a bug's life?

It can take a long time for an egg to develop into a winged adult. After this, however, an insect's life can be surprisingly brief. Sometimes there are only a few days or weeks to find a mate and breed so the species continues. Life is even shorter, of course, if predators are on the prowl. Some bugs spend months, even years, eating and growing as larvae. Periodic cicada nymphs live for 17 years deep underground, feeding on the nutrient-poor root sap of the tree where they began their lives as eggs.

Periodic cicada

Final molt of cicada nymph before it emerges as a fully grown adult

Q A How long is a butterfly's life?

Most adult butterflies live for only a few weeks, but some species, such as the peacock butterfly, can live for about a year by hibernating through the winter. They hide in hollow trees, cracks, and crevices to emerge in the spring, when they mate and lay their eggs.

Q A Which insect has the shortest life?

When mayflies emerge from the water as mature insects, they swarm together high in the air to mate. After the mayflies have dropped their eggs into the water, they survive only for a brief time. Adults have no mouths so cannot feed. Within a day, the mayflies die, their job done.

Large, striking eyespots to scare away predators

Peacock butterfly

Mayfly

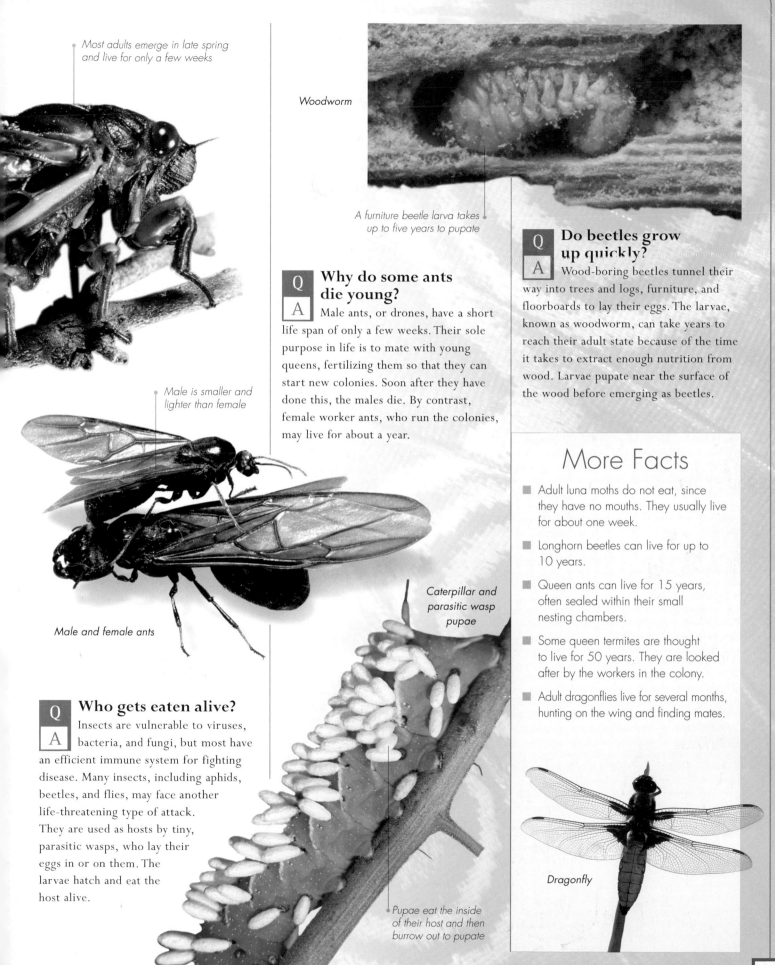

Most adults emerge in late spring and live for only a few weeks

Woodworm

A furniture beetle larva takes up to five years to pupate

Q A Do beetles grow up quickly?

Wood-boring beetles tunnel their way into trees and logs, furniture, and floorboards to lay their eggs. The larvae, known as woodworm, can take years to reach their adult state because of the time it takes to extract enough nutrition from wood. Larvae pupate near the surface of the wood before emerging as beetles.

Q A Why do some ants die young?

Male ants, or drones, have a short life span of only a few weeks. Their sole purpose in life is to mate with young queens, fertilizing them so that they can start new colonies. Soon after they have done this, the males die. By contrast, female worker ants, who run the colonies, may live for about a year.

Male is smaller and lighter than female

Male and female ants

More Facts

- Adult luna moths do not eat, since they have no mouths. They usually live for about one week.

- Longhorn beetles can live for up to 10 years.

- Queen ants can live for 15 years, often sealed within their small nesting chambers.

- Some queen termites are thought to live for 50 years. They are looked after by the workers in the colony.

- Adult dragonflies live for several months, hunting on the wing and finding mates.

Caterpillar and parasitic wasp pupae

Q A Who gets eaten alive?

Insects are vulnerable to viruses, bacteria, and fungi, but most have an efficient immune system for fighting disease. Many insects, including aphids, beetles, and flies, may face another life-threatening type of attack. They are used as hosts by tiny, parasitic wasps, who lay their eggs in or on them. The larvae hatch and eat the host alive.

Pupae eat the inside of their host and then burrow out to pupate

Dragonfly

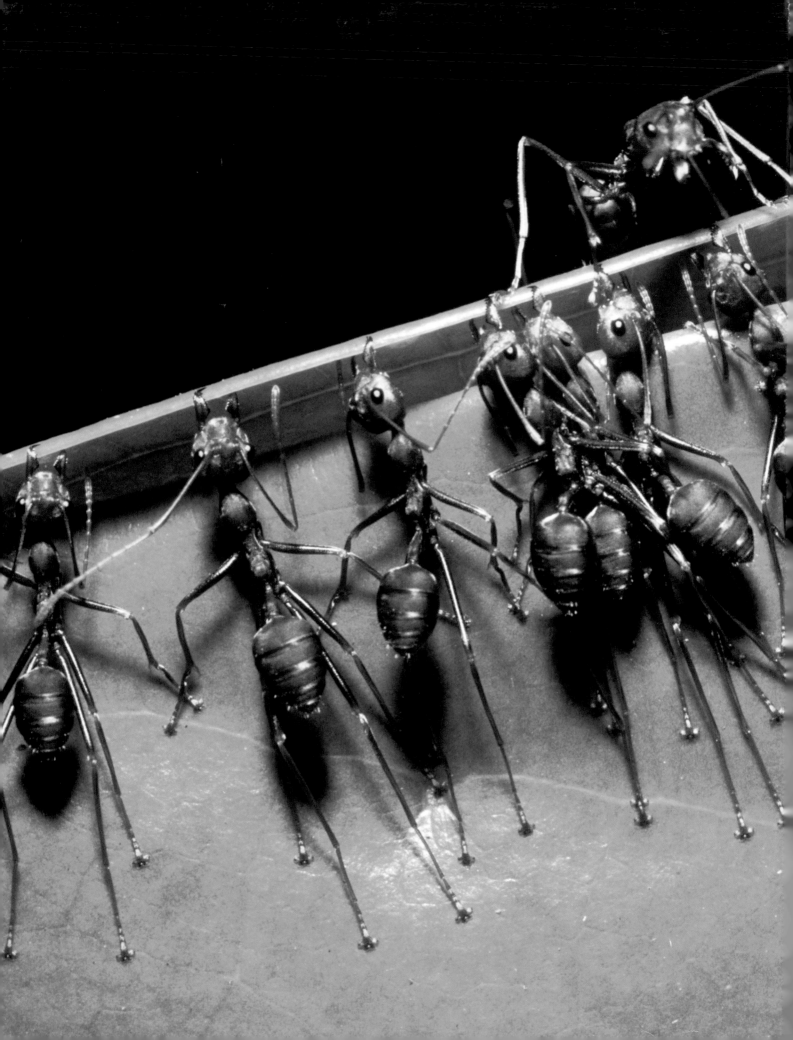

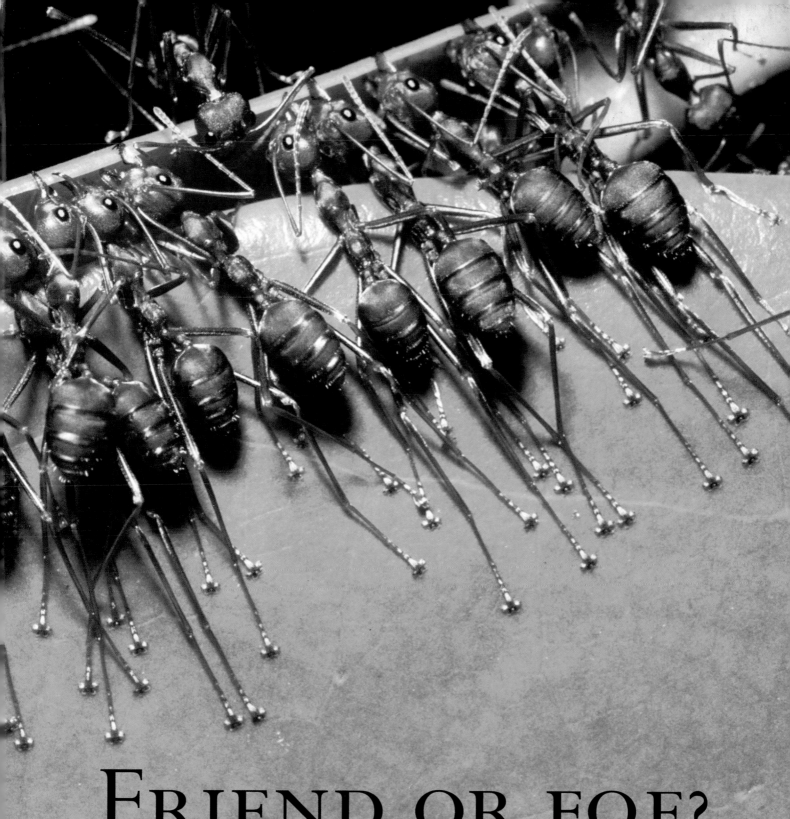

FRIEND OR FOE?

Which insects are helpful?

Although small—compared to other animals—insects play a large and important role in maintaining the natural balance of the ecosystem. They help in many ways, whether it's controlling pests and pollinating flowers, or recycling organic matter and improving the condition of the soil. They also provide a protein-rich source of food for birds, reptiles, small mammals, and even some plants. This ladybug is often referred to as the "gardener's friend" because it feeds on garden pests, such as aphids.

Ladybug and aphids

Aphids bite into the plant and suck huge amounts of sap

Q A Who likes to snack on snails?

Ground beetles usually hide during the day in leaf litter or under logs and come out at night to hunt their prey. Most species have powerful jaws and are fierce predators, helping to control a wide range of garden pests. Some feed on insect larvae, caterpillars, and pupae, and others eat slugs and snails.

Narrow head and elongated mouthparts for extracting food

Ground beetle

Q A How do insects help the ecosystem?

Earth-boring beetles help to aerate the soil and provide nutrients for it—by feeding on organic matter and breaking it down in their droppings. Dor beetles dig burrows deep underground and stock them with dung and dead or decaying plant matter to feed their larvae.

Dor beetle

Front legs have spikes for digging

More Facts

- Some wasps lay eggs inside aphids, where they hatch and mature, killing their hosts as they grow.

Silkworm cocoon

- A silkworm, which is the larva of the *Bombyx mori* moth, makes a cocoon from one long strand of silk that can measure up to 3,000 ft (900 m) when it is unraveled.

- The oldest record of people collecting honey from a bees' nest is a cave painting in Spain from about 9,000 years ago.

Q A Are insects good to eat?

They certainly provide food for many creatures—as well as for some plants. When an insect lands on the meat-eating Venus flytrap, it can trigger sensitive hairs on the leaves. The two halves of the trap then snap shut, trapping the unwary insect. Special juices from the plant then start to digest the insect prey.

Q A Which scavengers help to clean up?

Some species of fly, ant, and beetle are called scavengers, since they help to pick clean the decaying bodies of dead animals. They feed on rotting flesh and often lay their eggs on it. These quickly hatch into larvae, or maggots, which feed on the meat. Carrion beetles bury the carcasses of small vertebrates, like birds and rodents, as food for their larvae.

Wing cases protect hindwings when the beetles burrow under carrion (dead flesh)

Carrion beetle

Spines interlock to trap the struggling fly

Venus flytrap

Mosquito held with strong, toothed jaws

Dragonfly

Q A Are mosquitoes prey?

Dragonflies are strong and agile hunters and are sometimes called "mosquito hawks" because they can catch mosquitoes—as well as midges and other small flies. They can even make a basket out of their bristle-covered legs and scoop up prey in midair. In just one day, a dragonfly can eat 600 insects.

Jaws are tubular and curve forward

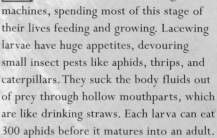

Lacewing larva

Q A Do larvae have big appetites?

Insect larvae are like eating machines, spending most of this stage of their lives feeding and growing. Lacewing larvae have huge appetites, devouring small insect pests like aphids, thrips, and caterpillars. They suck the body fluids out of prey through hollow mouthparts, which are like drinking straws. Each larva can eat 300 aphids before it matures into an adult.

What is pollination?

Plants need to be pollinated—or fertilized—so that they can reproduce, make seeds, and produce fruit. Flowers can sometimes pollinate themselves, but others need help to transfer pollen from their male to their female parts—or to another flower completely. Insects—bees in particular—are the great pollinators of the world and without them plant and animal life would be under threat. As this honey bee searches for nectar, its body is dusted with the pollen that will fertilize another flower.

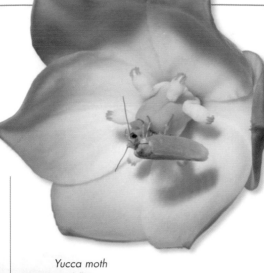

Yucca moth and flower

Q **A** **Can flowers be pollinated at night?**
The yucca plant, which grows in deserts, depends on a tiny, night-flying moth to pollinate its flowers. Without this insect, the plant could not reproduce itself. In turn, the moth depends on the plant, laying its eggs in the flowers. These hatch into larvae, which feed exclusively on yucca seeds.

White and yellow flowers are most attractive to bees

Honey bee

Body is covered with a fine dusting of pollen

Some pollen is stored in baskets on bee's hindlegs

How is pollen moved from plant to plant?

Honey bees visit many flowers to find nectar. The foragers, who are all female workers, fly from blossom to blossom, picking up pollen on their bodies as they go. They transfer it from one plant to another, which fertilizes them and enables them to bear fruit.

1 *The bee drinks nectar from inside the flower, hanging on tight with specially adapted feet.*

2 *As it feeds, the hairy body becomes covered with bright yellow pollen from the flower.*

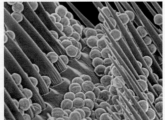

3 *Pollen is caught between hairs on the bee's body until it visits, and pollinates, another flower.*

Are butterflies good pollinators?

Butterflies are attracted to large, showy flowers that are bright red, orange, yellow, pink, or purple, and which often have a strong scent. They land on the petals and suck up the nectar from deep inside with their hollow tongues. But, unlike bees, they do not brush up against much pollen while feeding because their wings sit high above most of the flower.

Beetle on magnolia

Wings are folded as butterfly drinks nectar from flower

Beetle crawls into flower, gathering pollen on body

Red admiral butterfly

Do beetles ever pollinate plants?

Millions of years ago, flowers were pollinated by a range of insects, including beetles. Beetles tend to pollinate flowers that are dull white or green in color, often with a smell that is unpleasant to humans. Beetle-pollinated flowers include magnolia, aster, and rose.

Which insect helps to make chocolate?

A microscopic midge, about the size of a pinhead, pollinates the cacao tree. The flowers have both male and female parts but are not self-fertilizing. They rely on the midge to transport pollen for them. Large fruits—or pods—then develop, full of seeds, which are picked and manufactured into chocolate.

Cocoa midge

Midge lives in leaves on floor of rain forest

Cacao pod

Cacao seeds

Why do fig trees need wasps?

Each kind of fig tree is pollinated by its own particular species of wasp. The flowers and seeds of the tree grow together to form what looks like a fruit—or fig. The female wasp makes her way into the fig through a small opening. As she squeezes inside to lay her eggs, she brushes pollen from her body onto the female parts of the flower, which fertilizes them.

Antennae and wings sometimes torn off wasp when entering fig

Female fig wasp

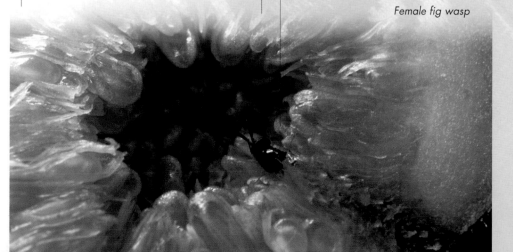

Who needs to feed on blood?

Some insects feed on plants, some eat other animals, dead or alive, and some are driven by the need to drink blood. These bloodsucking insects, which often emerge to feed at night, all have special mouthparts that can pierce skin and draw up blood. The female mosquito is probably the deadliest bloodsucker of all. Although she feeds on nectar and plant sap, she also needs to drink blood so that she can produce eggs. This insect carries and transmits serious diseases, including yellow fever and malaria.

Assassin bug

Q&A

Which bug has a deadly kiss?

Most members of the assassin bug family are expert hunters that prey on other insects. But one species, known as the kissing bug, feeds on the blood of small animals—and humans. These bugs come out from their hiding places at night and bite their sleeping victims on the soft flesh near the mouth.

Body of mosquito is slender and dull before feeding

Abdomen swells up and changes color as mosquito sucks up its blood meal

Mosquito

Long mouthpart for piercing skin and drinking blood

Mite on flea

Hedgehog

More Facts

- The color of a head louse is determined by the color of its host's hair.

- The best way to keep bloodsucking insects at bay is to eat garlic—the odor repels them.

- The female sand fly is a tiny gnat that sucks the blood of mammals, birds, and reptiles. She needs the protein to make her eggs.

- Maggots are sometimes used in modern medicine, since they eat dead tissue in wounds that will not heal and help to prevent gangrene.

- Bot flies lay their eggs on the mouth or face of sheep, cattle, and horses. These are licked off and swallowed. Larvae hatch in the gut, feeding and growing inside their host before emerging with the droppings.

Q A Who tries to hitch a ride?

Fleas spend most of their lives on host animals, like hedgehogs, feeding on their blood without killing them. Hedgehog fleas are specially adapted to living among the sharp spines of their host, although dog and cat fleas may hop on board for a short while. Sometimes mites hitch a ride on the flea. They cling on with the aid of tiny suckers.

Mite lives between the scales of the flea

Tsetse fly

Bodies are swollen after feeding

Bot fly larva

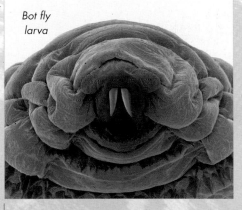

Q A Which flies suck blood?

Tsetse flies, found only in Africa, cause serious problems for both humans and animals. They are the size of large house flies and feed exclusively on blood. However, unlike most flies that bite, both males and females suck blood. These flies transmit a serious cattle disease, as well as sleeping sickness, which can be fatal to humans.

Q A What makes a flea flee?

Fleas spend most of their lives in the feathers or fur of warm-blooded animals, such as birds and mammals. From here, they can feed undetected on the blood of their host. They are capable of jumping vast distances to flee from danger or to jump from one host to another.

Bed bugs

Q A Is there a bug in the bed?

Bed bugs, which are oval, wingless insects, generally hide in cracks and crevices or in bedposts and mattresses during the day. They crawl out at night to drink blood. Before a meal, their bodies are brown and paper thin, but after feeding, they swell up and turn deep purple or red. Bed bugs need to drink blood once at each larval stage of growth.

Body has backward-pointing bristles to keep it from falling off host

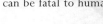

Flea

The energy that propels the flea on its giant jump is stored at the base of the legs

Who can be a real pest?

Insects such as this desert locust can cause devastation to crops and the people that rely on them. These pests take to the air in massive swarms and strip fields bare as they eat everything in their path. They can consume almost their own weight in food each day. Insects can also chew their way through floorboards, make holes in clothes, and invade kitchen cupboards. Some destroy plants and trees, while others cause serious damage across cotton fields and vineyards.

Biting, chewing mouthparts

Large compound eyes help with navigation

Young desert locust

Strong legs for marching through crop fields when too young to fly

Colorado beetles

Body has five brown stripes down each wing case

Q **A** **Which insect attacks potatoes?**
The Colorado beetle devours potato, tomato, and pepper plants. The female lays hundreds of eggs under the leaves of a plant. The eggs hatch soon after, and the larvae immediately start feeding. Colorado beetles were originally found in the Rocky Mountains of the US, but rapidly spread to Europe and Asia.

More Facts

- The adult common clothes moth does not eat during its lifetime, but its larvae can chew their way through carpets, clothes, and household furnishings.

Clothes moths

- House flies spit saliva onto solid food to break it down. They then suck up this soupy mess by using their soft, spongelike mouthparts.

- The confused flour beetle and red flour beetle are known as "bran bugs" because they feed on milled grain, such as flour and cereals.

- The bright red lily beetle may be pretty to look at, but its black larvae strip lily plants in days by feeding on the stems, foliage, and flowers.

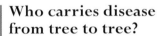

Q | A | Who carries disease from tree to tree?

Dutch elm disease has killed thousands of elm trees around the world. The disease is caused by a fungus, which is spread from tree to tree by elm bark beetles when they are feeding. The disease affects the tree's ability to transport water around its parts, and infected trees wilt rapidly.

Elm bark beetle and larvae

Grape berry moth caterpillar

Cream-colored caterpillar eats grape flesh

Q | A | Who is a vineyard pest?

Adult grape berry moths lay eggs on the underside of vine leaves. After hatching, the larvae set about eating the buds and blossoms on the vines. When the grapes grow bigger and juicier, the caterpillars tunnel their way deep inside to feed. Another insect pest, related to aphids, feeds on vine roots and leaves. The feeding causes galls to form on the developing leaves or roots.

Larva feeds for 8–10 days

Boll weevil on damaged cotton

Q | A | What is a boll weevil?

Weevils infest and ruin all kinds of important crops. The boll weevil is highly destructive, feeding on—and breeding in—the boll (fluffy seed pods) of the cotton plant. The female weevil lays about 200 eggs over a 10–12 day period in the bolls. She does this by drilling her way in with her long thin snout.

Galls form on grapevine leaf

Vine leaf

Q | A | Which pest protects itself with white wax?

Mealy bugs are part of the aphid family and are mainly found in warm countries and greenhouses. They drink the sap from a variety of plants, such as coffee trees, sugarcane, and citrus plants. To protect themselves as they drink, they secrete a layer of white, powdery wax. Only the females feed—but they can cause considerable damage.

Mealy bugs

Coating of powdery wax

INDEX

CREDITS

Dorling Kindersley would like to thank Jenny Finch for proof-reading and Steven Carton for editorial assistance.

The publisher would like to thank the following for their kind permission to reproduce their photographs:

Key: a=above; b=below/bottom; c=center; f=far; l=left; r=right; t=top

Agami Photo Agency: 37cla; **Alamy Images:** Heather Angel/Natural Visions 28 (main image); Bill Bachman 26l; Dave Bevan 17clb; Biodisc/Visuals Unlimited 13tr (closed spiracle); Blickwinkel/Hecker 38br; Blickwinkel/Kottmann 19cr, 45cla, 54br; Blickwinkel/Stahlbauer 38 (main image); Rick & Nora Bowers 43bl; Brand X Pictures 39cra; Scott Camazine 26crb, 36tr; Nigel Cattlin 58t, 59tc; Jeff Daly/Visuals Unlimited 36bl; John T. Fowler 53ca; Graphic Science 42tr, 52bl; Neil Hardwick 52br; Microscan/Phototake Inc. 33bc; Peter Arnold, Inc./David Scharf 19tc; Peter Arnold, Inc./Kevin Schafer 22br; Robert Pickett/Papilio 29tr; Mervyn Rees 55cl; Felipe Rodriguez 32bl; Runk/Schoenberger/Grant Heilman Photography 48t; Antje Schulte 37crb, 54l; Malcolm Schuyl 33cra; Sciencephotos 46tr; André Skonieczny/Imagebroker 44bl; Jack Thomas 25tr; Michael Weber/Imagebroker 35clb; Ian West 17cra; WILDLIFE GmbH 59tr; Christian Ziegler/Danita

Delimont 55br; **Ardea:** Pascal Goetgheluck 34b; 49tr; Chris Harvey 16br; Jean-Michel Labat 14cl; John Mason 24c; John Mason (JLMO) 15cra; **Bugwood. org:** Reyes Garcia III, USDA Agricultural Research Service 13crb; **Corbis:** Michael & Patricia Fogden 54tr; George D. Lepp/Documentary Value 59cb; **DK Images:** Thomas Marent 8-9, 15tc, 20-21, 23r, 30-31, 40-41, 46c, 47bl, 47cla; Natural History Museum, London 6bl, 10-11 (Alexander birdwing), 11tr, 14tr, 15tl, 23c, 34tr, 43c, 46bc, 48bl; Oxford Scientific Films 24-25; Jerry Young 11cb, 57tl; **FLPA:** Ingo Arndt/Minden Pictures 17crb; Richard Becker 39clb; Michael & Patricia Fogden/Minden Pictures 22tr; D. Jones 18tr; Rene Krekels/FN/Minden Pictures 33crb; Mark Moffett/Minden Pictures 26-27c, 42 (main image), 49cl; Piotr Naskrecki/Minden Pictures 45cr; **Getty Images:** Discovery Channel Images/Jeff Foott 39tl; Tim Flach/Stone+ 6-7bc; George Grall/National Geographic 5, 19br; Iconica/Tancrediphoto.com 54bl; The Image Bank/Art Wolfe 39br; The Image Bank/Ben Cranke 35cla; Photographer's Choice RR/Jeff Lepore 33tc; Science Faction/Bryan Reynolds 56b; Science Faction/Hans Pfletschinger 58bl; Skip Moody - Rainbow/Science Faction 7t; Taxi/Steve Hopkin 53bl; Visuals Unlimited/Boston Museum of Science 54fbr; Visuals Unlimited/Dr. Dennis Kunkel 57crb; Visuals Unlimited/Fritz Polking 53tl; Visuals Unlimited/Leroy Simon 35br; **Beatriz Moisset:** 55tc; **Natural Visions:** 13cra, 28crb; **naturepl.com:** Nature Production 23tc, 27tr; Premaphotos 50-51; Kim Taylor 36 (main image); Doug Wechsler 49bc; **NHPA/Photoshot:** A.N.T. Photo

Library 24bl, 27br; Anthony Bannister 43tl; George Bernard 15cl, 26br; N. A. Callow 25cb; Bill Coster 59br; Stephen Dalton 10bl, 29ca, 44br, 59bl; John Shaw 16tr, 17tfl, 17ftr, 17tl, 17tr; Martin Wendler 37tc; www.photo.antarctica.ac.uk: Peter Convey 22bl; **Photolibrary:** Animals Animals/Bill Beatty 53tr; Comstock/Creatas 4-5, 10-19 (background), 22-29 (background), 32-39 (background), 42-49 (background), 52-61 (background); Paul Freed 29cl; Oxford Scientific (OSF)/London Scientific Films 19clb; Oxford Scientific (OSF)/Mike Birkhead 59cla; Oxford Scientific (OSF)/Peter O'Toole 52cra; Oxford Scientific (OSF)/Satoshi Kuribayashi 43crb; **Science Photo Library:** Thierry Berrod, Mona Lisa Production 35tc; Dr. John Brackenbury 39c; Jeremy Burgess 57tc; Nigel Cattlin 16c; Steve Gschmeissner 53crb; Richard R. Hansen 23bc; Louise Murray 23clb; Bjorn Rorslett 32br, 32crb; Sinclair Stammers 56tr, 57clb; **Tom Murray:** 55cra; **Warren Photographic:** 24crb, 45bc.

Jacket images: Front: **Igor Siwanowicz**. Back: **Corbis:** Michael & Patricia Fogden fcl; Darrell Gulin fclb; Visuals Unlimited ftl; **Getty Images:** Altrendo Nature fcla; **Science Photo Library:** Stuart Wilson fbl. Spine: **DK Images:** Natural History Museum, London (butterfly x3); Jerry Young (red leaf beetle);
Front Endpapers: DK Images: Thomas Marent;
Back Endpapers: DK Images: Thomas Marent

All other images © Dorling Kindersley
For further information see: www.dkimages.com